Produced by Kroha Associates, Inc.
Middletown, Connecticut.

Printed in the United States of America.

ISBN 1-56326-112-X

# No Rumors
# Allowed!

Minnie was putting on her roller skates with the bright pink laces when Clarabelle called her on the phone.

"Hi, Minnie! I'm at Daisy's house. Can you come over and roller-skate with Daisy, Lilly, and me?" Clarabelle asked. "I have a pair of brand-new skates I want to show you."

"I'm skating with Penny," Minnie said. "Why don't we all skate together?"

"That would be fun," Clarabelle said, "but Daisy is kind of upset with Penny — she thinks Penny takes things that aren't hers!"

"That's not a very nice thing to say!" Minnie exclaimed.

"Well," Clarabelle went on, "that's what Daisy told Lilly, and what Lilly told me! Why would Daisy say something that isn't true?"

"I'm coming over to Daisy's right now to find out what all this is about!" Minnie said.

Minnie left a note for Penny and skated over to Daisy's house. Fifi trotted behind her. It was a warm fall day, but Minnie was too upset to notice the red and yellow leaves falling around her. She thought about the rumor Daisy had started. She was so worried, her usual smile turned upside-down into a funny little frown.

As Minnie skated up the walk, Lilly, Clarabelle, and Daisy were sitting on the front porch putting on their roller skates. When they saw Minnie, they smiled. But Minnie didn't feel like smiling back.

"What's wrong, Minnie?" Daisy asked. "You look worried."

"Why did you tell Lilly that Penny takes things that aren't hers?" Minnie asked.

"Because she took my new, shiny, purple coin purse," Daisy said. "I just got it last week. It was a birthday present from my Great-Aunt Dora."

"But how do you know Penny took it?" Minnie asked.

"Because," Daisy said, "yesterday Penny and I were roller-skating to the ice-cream store. I fell and hurt my knee, and we came back here to get a bandage. Then we decided to play dolls until it was time for Penny to go home. After she left, I couldn't find my coin purse anywhere. I'm really upset, because it had five dollars of my birthday money in it, too! I don't like saying it, but I'm sure Penny took my coin purse," Daisy admitted.

"How else would it have disappeared?" Lilly asked.

"Penny must have taken it," Clarabelle agreed.

"I don't care what you say," Minnie insisted. "I know Penny would *never* take your coin purse, Daisy."

Just then, Penny skated up to Daisy's front walk and waved at her friends. Only Minnie waved back.

"I got my allowance," Penny called. "Let's go get ice cream!"

"Uh, no thank you," said Daisy. "We're busy."

"Oh," Penny said softly.  She started to skate away, but Minnie
came after her.

"Wait, Penny!" she called.

"Why doesn't anyone want to come with me?" asked Penny sadly.
"Did I do something wrong?"

Minnie didn't know how to answer. For a minute she just stared at the ground. She was afraid to tell Penny what the other girls were saying about her. If Penny knew, it would hurt her feelings even more.

"Don't worry, Penny," Minnie said with a smile. "Everything will be all right, you'll see."

"I just want to go home," Penny said quietly. Minnie skated alongside her friend until they got to Penny's house, but neither girl felt like talking. Even Fifi seemed unhappy. Minnie watched Penny go inside.

" 'Bye!" Minnie called after her, trying to sound cheery — but Penny didn't turn around.

When Minnie got back to Daisy's house, everyone was skating up and down the sidewalk — but no one was smiling or laughing or talking to each other.

Finally Daisy said, "I know Penny is sad, but she was wrong to take my coin purse!"

"It's wrong to start rumors, too," Minnie told her. "You don't know for sure that Penny took your purse. Maybe you dropped it in the house when you came back to take care of your knee."

"I don't think so," Daisy answered. "I looked everywhere."

"Let's look again," Minnie suggested. So they all took off their skates and went inside to search some more.

Clarabelle peeked beneath the couch and under the cushions of the living room chairs.

Lilly searched the kitchen counters and inside all the drawers.

Daisy and Minnie peered under Daisy's bed and behind her dresser.
But no one found Daisy's coin purse.

"Maybe you dropped your coin purse in the yard," Minnie suggested.

So all the girls went outside and spread out. They looked in the grass. They searched the flower bed and looked inside the mailbox. They shined a flashlight under the porch, but all they found was a spider web and a sleepy spider. What they didn't find was Daisy's coin purse.

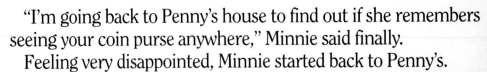

"I'm going back to Penny's house to find out if she remembers seeing your coin purse anywhere," Minnie said finally.

Feeling very disappointed, Minnie started back to Penny's. She walked slowly, scuffing her feet through the pretty leaves on the sidewalk. Fifi trailed behind Minnie with her tail drooping.

Suddenly, Fifi stopped walking and began to dig excitedly in a big pile of leaves. Minnie ran up beside her. "Fifi, what is it?" Minnie cried as she knelt down beside her.

There, at the bottom of the pile, was Daisy's new, shiny, purple coin purse! Minnie crossed her fingers for good luck. Then she opened the purse and peeked inside.

"Hurrah!" Minnie yelled. There were five crisp, new, one-dollar bills neatly folded inside.

"Good girl, Fifi!" Minnie said, and she gave her dog a big hug.

Minnie ran all the way back to Daisy's house with Fifi barking happily beside her. "Daisy, look!" she called. "Fifi and I found your coin purse under some leaves on the sidewalk. And your money is still in it!"

"Oh, thank goodness!" Daisy exclaimed. "I must have dropped it when I fell and hurt my knee roller-skating. I'm so happy that you found it!"

Then Daisy clapped her hand over her mouth. "Golly, I've made a terrible mistake," she cried. "I told everyone Penny took my coin purse. I have to apologize to her right now!"

Daisy ran to Penny's house as fast as she could. Minnie and the others were right behind her.

Penny was teary-eyed when she answered the door.

"Penny, I did something that wasn't very nice," Daisy blurted out. "I told everyone you took my coin purse and money."

"Oh, no!" Penny said, but Daisy kept right on talking. "Minnie found my coin purse. She showed me I was wrong to say those things about you. I'm so sorry! I'll tell everyone the truth, I promise. Will you forgive me?"

"I — I guess so," Penny said slowly.

"I have an idea," Minnie said, and she whispered it to Daisy. Daisy nodded and smiled. "Come on, Penny," she said as she took her friend's hand. "Let's go get those ice-cream cones we didn't get last time. I'll treat with the money I got for my birthday!"

Soon the five friends were enjoying chocolate ice-cream cones. Everyone was happy, especially Penny.

"Now I'm going to start a rumor," Penny said with a grin.

"Oh, no!" they all shouted.

"Don't!" Daisy said. "I've learned that starting rumors makes a mess of everything!"

"But this is a good rumor," Penny said as she winked at Minnie. "I'm going to tell everyone that Minnie — and Fifi — are the best friends anyone could ever have!"

"Arf! Arf!" agreed Fifi, and they all laughed.

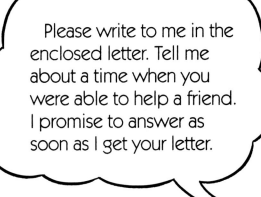